What do they

Eat?

Volume 2

By Lyla & Danny Fitzsimmons

For my sister Mia....

Bees like nectar...

Bears like honey...

Now you know what
they eat..

Pandas like bamboo...

Snakes like mice...

Now you know what
they eat..

Tortoise like ...

Pigs like truffles...

Now you know what
they eat..

Cats like cat food...

Moles like worms ...

Now you know what they eat..

Alpacas like hay...

Anteaters like ants...

Now you know what they eat..

Crabs like algae...

My Mummy likes chocolate...

Now you know what they eat..

Can you match these animals to the

13

food they eat?

Here's some food and drink to make

Grapes

Fruit Smoothie

Corn

Tomato

Potato

us humans
Big and Strong...

Fish

Porridge

Water

Eggs

Strawberries

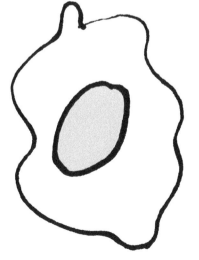

The End